# A Christmas in Yellowstone

Written by **Kathryn Phyllarry**

Illustrated by **Robert Rath**

Homestead Publishing

Moose, WY • San Francisco, CA

*T*o all the wildlife in Yellowstone National Park,

may your treasures be many and your challenges be few.

Copyright © 2015 by Kathryn Rittmueller

Book design by Robert Rath

ISBN 978-0-943972-85-5

Library of Congress Control Number 2010929288

First Edition
Printed in China

Published by
Homestead Publishing
Box 193 • Moose, Wyoming
& San Francisco, California

For other fine Homestead titles, please contact:
Mail Order Department
Homestead Publishing
Box 193 • Moose, Wyoming 83012
or www.homesteadpublishing.net

*I*t is winter in Yellowstone and no human visitors roam.

This is a challenging season to call this place home.

*W*ith mountains wrapped in ice and snow,
Yellowstone is a place that few people know.

$\mathcal{D}$etails of the land quickly disappear,

and for wildlife that are not hibernating,

it is a difficult time of year.

But in a valley, in the forest, a mystery brews,

and to all the wildlife, its magic it woos.

A new, thermal pool out of nowhere appears,

and its brooding steam no animal fears.

*E*very variety of wildlife that are not asleep,

from the whistling pikas to the big horn sheep,

all come to the pool to watch and listen

as the snowflakes fall and the water glistens.

*T*here are bison, coyotes, trumpeter swans and ducks...

$\mathcal{R}$ed fox and mule deer: fawns, does and bucks.

The elk, wolves, porcupines and snowshoe hares
all venture out of their winter lairs.

*A*ntelope, bald eagles, moose and otters

fly or trudge through the snow to the curious water.

When the gurgling thermal begins to erupt,
quills, feathers and fur stand up.

_T_hen suddenly the pool opens and it begins to speak,

and not one animal utters a peep.

"Winter is a time all of you want to rest,

but hunger pulls you from your warm cozy nests.

I want all of you to hunt, burrow and scour

for something out there that gives you more power

to ride out the winter, Yellowstone's ultimate test,

and show Mother Nature who is the best."

"But listen well my friends, there is one simple rule,
you must bring a piece of it to this mystical pool."

"On December 25th, a magical day of the year,

you will deliver your treasures and look into my mirror.

You will find something special, something unique;

it will definitely be something each of you seek."

$A$s the steam rises and the water bubbles,

the animals feel they have fewer troubles.

This wonderful pool will fix their problems in life,

and the cold, icy winter can be faced without strife.

The animals leave with hope in their hearts
to investigate Yellowstone's far reaching parts.
They will search for treasures that give power and reason
to ride out Mother Nature's toughest of seasons.

The pikas set out to find lichens that are sweet.

In the dead of winter, this is a feat.

They all work together and low and behold;

they find special lichens more precious than gold.

*F*or the bighorn sheep finding a salt lick is their aim,

and they discover a dried mineral pool to claim.

Since deep, heavy snow bogs bison down,

they set out to find unique snow-free ground

where both vegetation and a warm bed abound.

*T*hey lumber along with steps that don't hasten

and eventually find a warm geyser basin

where misty grasses hang with dew,

and Oh, what a spectacular view.

$F$or wolves, the test is by far the hardest

because they have to travel the farthest.

The pack leaves the park and its wildlife protection

to find something to eat without man's detection

With roving eyes, they search high and low,
and suddenly, spy something beside an oxbow.

There are meat piles left by hunters that humans don't eat
but to hungry wolves are a delicious treat.

The coyotes and fox head to a snow-covered meadow

where they patiently listen and crawl very low

to hear mice running beneath the snow....

*T*o wait for the moment to dive deep below.

Each of them have a snow-covered snout,

but a new mouse den they are successful to rout.

$\mathcal{T}$rumpeter swans and ducks find warm, thermal rivers

that stay open in winter and prevent the shivers.

There is plenty to eat since the waters never freeze,
and feathered friends can doze with ease.

*T*he snowshoe hares and porcupines

have better luck finding places to dine.

There are twigs and bark from lodge pole pines

which suit both of their diets just fine.

*I*f that isn't enough, they can burrow and dig

to find precious roots both little and big.

*M*oose and elk stay away from snow that is deep

so the thick, fat layers in their bodies they can keep.

They find dry grasses beneath their feet,

and when these are not around, dormant, tree limbs are a treat.

*I*n winter, deer and antelope set a much slower pace.

They never set out on a summer like chase.

*L*ike the moose and elk, grasses suit their tastes,

and few frozen blades ever go to waste.

But what is this they see up ahead?

Sagebrush is sticking out of its snow-covered bed,

and this they will feast on instead.

*O*nce they finish eating the uncovered tops,

they start to dig until the ground makes them stop.

The effort reveals cherished sagebrush twig,

and the extra work is well worth the dig.

$\mathcal{T}$he bald eagles fly off to a vast, frozen plane,

but actually, Yellowstone Lake is its name.

The lake freezes over but wildlife know how

to catch cutthroat trout swimming below.

The warm, steamy water around the edge of the lake
bubbles and churns for breather holes to make.

*T*his open edge is the perfect spot

to soar, high above and devise a plot.

*A*t the edge of a hole romp well fed otters,

who surface from beneath the misty waters.

In the mouth of one is a fat, juicy fish,

this is a wonderful, afternoon dish.

$\mathcal{T}$hen suddenly, with a wiggle and flip,

the fish escapes the otter's firm grip.

An eagle above sees an opportunity to make,

and he takes advantage of the otter's mistake.

$W$ith wide, sweeping wings, the eagle flies down
and snatches the fish without making a sound.

$\mathcal{D}$isappointed, the otter dives back in the hole,

to find the plumpest fish is his goal.

$\mathcal{T}$o the otter's amazement, his next catch is a winner.

As he surfaces with his lip-smacking dinner,

the others scan the skies

with watchful eyes.

This time his meal, fit for a king,

will not fly off beneath an eagle's wing.

As the wildlife feast on their precious finds,
they keep a thought in the back of their minds.
A piece of every scrumptious meal
must go to the pool that is the deal.

$O$n December 25th, the animals brave the cold

to reach the mystic water as the pool had foretold.

All the animals think the pool will triple their treasures,

and their species will be fed in bountiful measure.

They will win this hard-fought test

and reign victorious over the rest.

$A$s they place their priceless finds in the pool,

the water sparkles like a twinkling jewel.

$\mathcal{T}$hen suddenly the pool begins to erupt.

It's like a crayon box of blue and silver as it lights up.

$I$t is a breathtaking steam of natural wonder,

but the animals question if they made a big blunder.

*W*hen magically, between the fog and diamond dust,

there appears an unusual, icicle crust,

and it captures every animal's trust.

*T*hen a brilliant star shines over their heads
and glittering words can be read.

"PEACE ON EARTH AND GOOD WILL TO ALL LIVING THINGS;"
is the message seen through warm, steamy rings.

*I*n an instant, the fog and shimmering words disappear,

and the pool dries up; there is no glossy mirror.

$A$s the star continues to shine its bright light,

the wildlife realize something tonight.

*W*hen they look deep into everyone's face,

they realize the beauty of this place,

and finally, hear voices other than their own

who call this magnificent park their home.

Each species passes the hard-fought test,

and no one is any better than the rest.

*I*n the light of this beautiful, shining star,
the warm days of summer don't seem far.
The pool gives strength to find the way
to meet winter's challenges every day.

*L*ike the miracle star so long ago

that brought peace and harmony to those below,

it guided the way to a lowly manger

to meet God's, perfect, little stranger.

Peace on earth and

Although thousands of years apart,

both stars put strength in all living hearts.

# Goodwill to all living things

*T*hey shine down and give reasons to cope

and fill both worlds with miraculous hope.

*K*athryn (Jensen) Rittmueller, whose pseudonum is Kathryn Phyllarry, is the author of Moon Beam award-winner *Beauregart the Bear*, *A Goose Tale: Gwen and Gabe's Journey* and *Flames, Friends and The Miracle in Yellowstone*. She lives with her husband in Wyoming.